Why Tortoise Has a Cracked Shell

Retold by Jane Langford

Illustrated by Joanna Isles

Heinemann

Chapter 1

Long, long ago, when the world had just begun, all the animals met in the jungle. They sat round in a big circle.

They were very sad. They each didn't know how they should move or how they should talk.

'Who is going to tell us what to do?' asked Crow.

'No one,' said Tortoise. 'We have to make up our own minds.'

But it was very hard to do. None of the animals had been on the Earth very long.

Snake was brave. 'I'll go first,' he said. 'I think I know how to move.'

Everybody watched Snake. He stood on the end of his tail and hopped.

'How does that feel?' asked Cat.

'Terrible!' said Snake. 'My tail hurts.'

Snake tried again. He curled
up in a loop and spun like a
spinning top.

'Now, how do you feel?'
asked Cat.

'Dizzy!' said Snake. 'I think I'm
going to fall over.'

Snake did just that. He fell
over and could not get up again.
He slithered all over the ground.

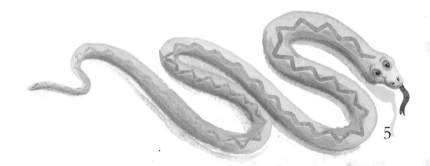

'That looks a good way to move!' said Cat.

'Does it?' said Snake.

Snake slithered again. It was fun. He slithered up and down the jungle paths and was very happy.

'This is ss-super!' he hissed. 'Ss-slithering is ss-simply ss-splendid!'

All the other animals agreed. They liked the way Snake slithered. They liked the way he hissed.

Monkey jumped up and down.
'I want to go next,' he said.
'I want to learn how to move.'
Everybody laughed.
'You already know how to move!' said Cat. 'You are jumping up and down like a Yo-Yo.'

7

Monkey was amazed.

'I am jumping! I am!' he said. 'But it's not enough. I want to jump in the trees. I want to swing in the branches.'

'Then try it,' said Crow.

Monkey did just that. He jumped into a tree and swung from branch to branch. He was so excited that he started to jabber.

'Ee-ee! This is ee-ee-easy!'

Everybody was pleased. Snake could hiss and slither. Monkey could jump and jabber.

'Who's next?' asked Crow.

'Me!' said Cat. 'Me me me-ow!'

Everybody stood still. Everybody listened.

'Say that again,' said Crow.

Cat meowed again, 'Me me me-ow.'

'That's a lovely sound!' said Snake.

Cat was pleased. She was so pleased that she purred, 'Prrr, prrr.'

'Now, how are you going to move?' asked Crow.

Cat shook her head. She did not know.

'Show me how you would catch your supper,' said Crow.

Cat did just that. She hunched up her shoulders and padded along on her soft paws.

'You're prowling!' said Crow.

'Am I?' said Cat.

'Yes,' said Crow.

Everybody was pleased. Snake could hiss and slither. Monkey could jump and jabber. Cat could purr and prowl.

'Whose turn is it next?' asked Tortoise.

Everybody looked at Alligator. He was swishing his tail impatiently.

'Do you want to go next?' asked Crow.

Alligator was bad-tempered. He had waited a long time for his turn. He snapped his teeth at Crow. It made a loud sound.

Click!

Clack!

Click!

'That can be your sound,'
said Crow.

Alligator liked his sound. He
snapped his teeth and swished
his tail.

He nearly knocked Cat into
the water.

'Don't do that!' said Cat. 'I
don't like water!'

'I do!' said Alligator.

He slid into the water, swished
his tail and swam.

Everybody was very happy.
Snake could slither and hiss.
Monkey could jump and jabber.
Cat could purr and prowl.
Alligator could snap and swish.

Soon there were only two
animals left who didn't know how
to move or talk. They were
Tortoise and Crow.

Chapter 2

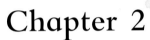

All the animals gathered round
Crow and Tortoise.

'It's your turn now,' said Cat.
'You have to decide how to move.'

'You could swing through the
trees, like me,' said Monkey.

'You could swim in the water,
like me,' said Alligator.

'You could ss-slither over the
ground, like me,' hissed Snake.

'Or prowl through the long
grass, like me,' said Cat.

Tortoise and Crow shook their heads. They knew they did not want to move like any of the other animals. But they did not know how they DID want to move.

Tortoise disappeared inside his shell to think. Crow shook his feathers and went to sleep.

Everybody began to get impatient. The sun was going down and the jungle was beginning to feel cool. Soon it would be night.

'Hurry up,' hissed Snake. 'Surely you have some idea of how you want to move?'

Tortoise popped his head back out of his shell. Crow woke up.

'I want to be special,' said Tortoise. 'I want to move in a really special way.'

'I want to be special too,' said Crow.

The animals looked at Tortoise. They looked at Crow.

'You are already special,' said Cat to Tortoise. 'You have a beautiful shell. It is smooth and shiny, like polished glass.'

All the other animals agreed. Everyone loved Tortoise's shell. It was like a mirror. Crow could see himself in Tortoise's shell.

'I am not special,' said Crow. 'I am ugly. Look at my horrible black feathers.'

'Feathers are wonderful,' said Alligator. 'They keep you warm. I wish I had feathers.'

'Feathers are beautiful,' said Monkey. 'Your black feathers are long and shiny.'

'Feathers are very ss-special,' hissed Snake. 'If you have feathers, you can fly.'

All the animals looked at Snake. They had never heard of flying before.

'What is flying?' asked Cat.

'It is floating through the air,' said Snake.

'How can I float through the air?' asked Crow.

'It's easy,' said Snake. 'You flap your wings up and down and soar into the air. You float in the breeze and glide through clouds.'

'That sounds wonderful!' said Crow. 'I think I want to fly.'

'I want to fly too!' said Tortoise. 'Flying sounds like fun.'

Everyone looked at Tortoise. They looked at his beautiful shiny shell. They looked at his stubby little legs.

'You haven't got wings,' said Cat.

'You haven't got feathers,' said Crow.

'That doesn't matter,' said Tortoise. 'I'm sure I can fly.'

'Let's practise,' said Crow.

'All right,' said Tortoise. 'How do we begin?'

Snake slithered on to a rock.

'You ss-start off by running,' he hissed, 'then you flap your wings.'

'Yes,' said Crow, 'then what happens?'

Snake slithered over his rock. 'You take off,' he said.

Crow and Tortoise tried. They ran along the dusty ground. Crow flapped his big black wings. Tortoise flapped his stubby legs.

'It's not working!' shouted Crow.

'It's not working!' panted Tortoise.

'You need more practice,' said Cat.

'You need to go faster,' said Snake.

Crow went faster. So did Tortoise.

'There must be something else,' said Crow. 'It's still not working.'

Snake was puzzled. He was sure that flying was a good way to move. 'I know!' he said. 'It works better if you start off from somewhere very high.'

Crow and Tortoise stopped running.

'That's it!' said Crow. 'If we find somewhere very high, we can just jump off! We'll be flying in no time.'

'Perfect!' said Tortoise. 'That's exactly what we will do.'

Chapter 3

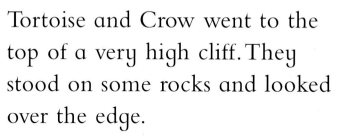

Tortoise and Crow went to the top of a very high cliff. They stood on some rocks and looked over the edge.

'It's a very long way down,' said Crow.

'That doesn't matter,' said Tortoise. 'You don't have to look down. When we start to fly, we will go up.'

Crow looked up into the sky. The sun was setting over the jungle. The clouds were pink and orange.

'Isn't it beautiful up there?'
Crow said. 'I can't wait to fly.'

'Nor can I,' said Tortoise.
'Let's go.'

Crow rushed towards the edge.
'I'll go first. You can watch how I
flap my wings.'

'All right,' said Tortoise. He
waved to the other animals. They
were waiting at the bottom of the
cliff. 'We're ready!' he shouted.
'Crow is going to be first!'

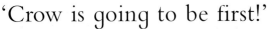

Crow stood a little way back from the edge. He held his head up high and looked at the clouds.

'I'm going to go up, not down,' he said.

Crow took a deep breath and spread his wings out wide. 'I'm ready!' he shouted.

'Good luck!' said Tortoise.

Crow ran towards the edge of the cliff. For a moment, he seemed to stay in mid-air.

Then he started to drop.

'Flap your wings!' shouted
Tortoise. 'You've forgotten to flap
your wings.'

Crow flapped his wings. He
could feel his feathers pushing
against the air. He flapped harder.

'You're flying!' shouted Tortoise.

'Caw!' shouted Crow. 'Caw!
Caw! Caw! This is wonderful!'

'And now you've found your
special way of talking too,'
shouted Cat.

Tortoise could not wait any longer. He wanted to fly like Crow. He took a step back from the edge and then he launched himself into the air.

'I'm flying!' he said.

He flapped his stubby legs as hard as he could.

'No you're not!' shouted
Alligator.

'No you're not!' shouted Snake.

'No you're not!' shouted Crow.

Monkey and Cat could not
bear to look. They covered their
eyes with their paws.

Tortoise fell through the air. His beautiful shiny shell was too heavy. His short stubby legs did not work like wings.

'I haven't got any feathers!' shouted Tortoise. 'I haven't got any wings!'

'We know!' shouted the animals. 'We know!'

Tortoise tumbled and tumbled. It was a very long way down.

At last he hit the ground.

THUMP! CRASH!

Snake slithered over to him.

'Are you all right?' he asked.

Tortoise shook his head. 'No,' he said, 'look at my shell.'

Snake looked at Tortoise's shell. It was broken into a hundred pieces. Each piece glinted in the setting sun.

Tortoise started to cry. His beautiful shell was broken.

'What shall I do?' he sobbed.

'Don't worry,' said Cat. 'We will mend you.'

'Yes-ss,' hissed Snake, 'of course we will.'

Cat and Snake picked up all the pieces of Tortoise's shell. They put them back together. Soon Tortoise looked as good as new – well, almost.

'How do I look?' asked Tortoise.

'Strange,' said Crow.

'Different,' said Snake.

'Special!' said Cat.

Tortoise's shell was back in one piece, but it wasn't smooth and shiny any more. It was lumpy and bumpy and cracked. It looked as if it might fall apart again.

'How shall I move now?' asked Tortoise.

'Very slowly and carefully,' said Crow.

Tortoise couldn't think of anything to say. But if you ever see him, you will find that he has taken Crow's advice.

And to this day, he still can't think of anything to say.